Brayden's Magical Jungle

Anita A. Caruso

A.A. Caruso

Brayden's Magical Jungle, Published July, 2015

Cover and Interior Illustrations: Randy Jennings
Interior Design & Layout: Howard Johnson, Howard Communigrafix, Inc.
Editorial and Proofreading: Lisa Ann Schleipfer, Eden Rivers Editorial Services; Karen Grennan
Photo Credits: Anita A. Caruso

 SDP Publishing

Published by SDP Publishing, an imprint of SDP Publishing Solutions, LLC.

For more information about this book contact Lisa Akoury-Ross at SDP Publishing by email at info@SDPPublishing.com.

To obtain permission(s) to use material from this work, please submit a written request to:

SDP Publishing
Permissions Department
PO Box 26
East Bridgewater, MA 02333
or email your request to info@SDPPublishing.com.

ISBN-13 (print): 978-0-9964345-1-5

ISBN-13 (ebook): 978-0-9964345-2-2

Printed in the United States of America

To my great-grandson,
Brayden.
May you always have magic in your life.

Six-year-old Brayden lived in a three-level house on Blueberry Lane. It was larger than any house in the neighborhood. Brayden's bedroom was on the top floor, which overlooked a big, empty field.

Brayden loved all of his stuffed animals. There was Levi Lion, Tyler Tiger, Griffin Giraffe, Elijah Elephant, and two monkeys, Marley and Max. Brayden often looked out his bedroom window and wished he lived in the jungle with his animal friends.

The big, empty field was separated from Brayden's house by high, thick bushes. Brayden always wondered how far this field went. "My mother does not want me to go into the field," he remembered. "She thinks I will get lost."

One day, while his mom was in the kitchen, Brayden tiptoed out the side door and headed for the bushes. He found a small opening in them and crawled into the empty field. He knew his mother would not be happy, but he was a curious little boy.

As he walked further into the field the grass was high to his waist. The field was much bigger than he thought. As he walked along Brayden tripped and fell. There in the grass was a pair of green sunglasses.

Brayden picked them up and jumped to his feet. They were much too big for his small face, but the sun was so bright he decided to put them on. Suddenly he was standing in the middle of a jungle.

Brayden quickly took them off and found himself back in the empty field. When he put them on again, he was back in the jungle. He looked around.

"These glasses are magic," he whispered to himself. His wish had come true. He could feel his heart beating. Did anybody live here? Was he alone?

Then he heard a squeaky voice call out, "Hello there! I'm Percy Parrot. Welcome to our jungle."

Brayden looked up and saw a big parrot perched on a tree branch. He was so colorful with green, yellow, and red feathers. He even had an orange beak.

"I'm Brayden. I'm six years old and I live next door."

"Well, I don't know where *next door* is," Percy Parrot said, "but we've been expecting you. All your animal friends are here and want to have fun with you."

Just then Levi Lion and Tyler Tiger came leaping and roaring out of the jungle bushes so loudly that it made the grasses sway back and forth like waves in an ocean.

"Hey, Brayden! You have to look up to see me," said
Griffin Giraffe.

"Watch out!" Thundering down the path was Elijah Elephant. He scooped Brayden up with his trunk onto his back, and Brayden squealed with delight. Then two monkeys swung past him, going from tree to tree and giving him a friendly pat on the top of his head.

"That's Marley and Max," said Percy Parrot.

"All of you live in my bedroom back home! Not you, Percy Parrot!" cried Brayden.

"This is a magical jungle and I am going to be your guide," said Percy Parrot. "I am going to show you how to have fun with your animal friends."

Then Marley Monkey and Max Monkey each took one of Brayden's arms and swooped him up to a tree branch. Then all three of them swung from one tree to another. Brayden wasn't scared at all. He loved being one of the monkeys.

"Hey, Brayden! Are you hungry?" asked Marley Monkey.

"Yes," Brayden answered. "I haven't eaten since breakfast."

Marley Monkey swung Brayden to a huge, flat rock below while Max
Monkey tossed bananas that fell by Brayden's feet. The rock was
so big that all three friends were able to sit together while happily
munching bananas.

Looking up, Brayden saw Griffin Giraffe munching on juicy, red berries from one of the tall bushes. "Ooh, can I have some berries?" squealed Brayden. So Elijah Elephant again lifted Brayden up with his trunk, and this time placed him gently onto the giraffe's back.

20

"Whee!" exclaimed Brayden. "Look at me! I'm way up high. I can almost touch the sky!"

Then he looked down to see Levi Lion and Tyler Tiger running in circles, each trying to roar louder than the other. With all that roaring Levi became tired.

"Hey, everyone! I am going to take a nap. We lions usually sleep during the day and are up at night. I am off to sleep in the grasses. See you all later!"

Elijah Elephant placed Brayden down on the ground. Brayden said, "I'm thirsty."

"I'll take you to the river," Tyler Tiger roared.

After taking off his shoes and socks, Brayden splashed with his feet while drinking the water. Then Tyler Tiger jumped into the river splashing himself all over. "We tigers love to swim. Watch me!"

Brayden thought he looked silly.

After awhile Tyler Tiger climbed onto the riverbank. The new friends rested on the grass under the hot, sunny sky. Brayden curled up next to the sleepy Tyler Tiger and they both fell asleep.

When Brayden woke up he saw that the sun had disappeared and darkness had set in. He woke Tyler Tiger up. "We have slept too long and must go back and find the others," said Brayden.

They returned to the spot where Brayden first arrived in the jungle.

"I'm having so much fun. I don't want to go home, but I have to right away," Brayden said.

"No! No!" they cried back. "You can't go yet. We have to play some more."

"Don't worry, I will come back," he said in a loud voice. And with that he took his glasses off.

Brayden was standing back in the field. "I am going to miss my jungle friends," he thought as he looked over his shoulder. "They are gone now, but I had so much fun with them."

Right now Brayden knew he needed to hurry home. "My mom and dad are going to be mad at me," he thought.

Then Brayden saw that the sun was shining. "Why isn't it nighttime?" Brayden thought. "It was when I left the jungle."

Not wasting a moment he began running toward home as fast as his little legs could carry him, but he could not remember where the space in the bushes was that he had crawled through earlier. "Where is the opening?" he cried as he raced along all the tall bushes. Just then he saw a brightly colored feather lying on the ground. "How did this get here?" he wondered. As he looked up he saw the opening in the bushes.

Brayden tried to be quiet sneaking into the house, but his mother heard the squeaking of the door. "Is that you, Dear? It is time for lunch. Do not forget to wash your hands."

"Lunch! It is only lunchtime," Brayden thought. He could not believe what had happened. "It must have something to do with my magic sunglasses," he thought.

Before washing his hands, he decided to go to his bedroom and check on his animal friends. "I have to find a safe place to hide my sunglasses," he thought. Seeing the zipper on Levi Lion's back gave him an idea.

"I will put the glasses inside Levi's back. My mother will never look there," he thought.

"I will be back to see you in the jungle soon," he whispered to Levi Lion. "This will be our secret."

As he washed his hands for lunch Brayden thought about his magic glasses and wondered what other kinds of adventures he could have with them. He laughed to himself as he scampered down the stairs to the kitchen.

This was surely his lucky day!

About The Author

Anita Ann Caruso was a former interior designer for more than 40 years and the author of the memoir, *"As Ever, Pudd:" A Love Story That Never Ends Told in Letters*. From the age of 10 her imagination loved to create fun stories and exciting adventures. Being a grandmother to her 31 grandchildren and 14 great-grandchildren inspired her to write her children's book.

Brayden's Magical Jungle is the first in a series of Brayden's Magical Journey books. In each subsequent book Brayden will be teamed up with some of his cousins. "With these many great-grandchildren, and I'm sure, more to come, Brayden's magical journey possibilities are endless," Anita says.

Anita has lived on Cape Cod for 49 years.

Brayden's Magical Jungle
Anita A. Caruso

www.anitaacarusobooks.com

Also available in ebook format

TO PURCHASE:

Amazon.com

BarnesAndNoble.com

SDPPublishing.com

SDP Publishing

www.SDPPublishing.com

Contact us at: info@SDPPublishing.com

CPSIA information can be obtained at www.ICGtesting.com
Printed in the USA
BVOW10s2355140715

408824BV00005B/5/P